If you rec

ELEPHANT PANTS

For Gabriel and Rafi, with love – S.P-H.

For Tara, with love – D.W.

ORCHARD BOOKS
338 Euston Road, London NW1 3BH
Orchard Books Australia
Level 17/207 Kent Street, Sydney, NSW 2000

First published in 2012 by Orchard Books

A CIP catalogue record for this book is available from the British Library.

ISBN 978 1 40831 347 3

1 3 5 7 9 10 8 6 4 2

Printed in China

Orchard Books is a division of Hachette Children's Books,
an Hachette UK company.
www.hachette.co.uk

ELEPHANT PANTS

Smriti
Prasadam-Halls

ORCHARD

David
Wojtowycz

The ark was peaceful, no sound could be heard,

No noise from animal, insect or bird.

Till a cry ripped the air,

"Oh, fiddle-dee fickers,

Where, oh where, oh

WHERE are my knickers?"

"Major Trump?
What in heaven's name is the matter?"
Called Noah amidst all the
clamour and clatter.

"My undies are missing – they're just like these.

Oh, Noah, will you help me locate them,
PLEASE?"

"Don't worry, it's an easy muddle to make,

Maybe someone's put them on by mistake.

ARK ALERT!" called Noah.

"Come, gather round,

There are missing pants . . .

and they need to be found!

Please could each animal

line up to display,

The pants

they've decided to put on today.

And should you all follow this kind request,

We'll soon lay the

missing pants mystery to rest!"

The hippos went first with a
sniff and a snort.

"Yes, very nice, but they're not the right sort."

The giraffes showed boxers
with buttons and bows . . .
"No offence, but I wouldn't be seen in those!"

The flamingos said,

"Frankly we're most unimpressed

To be ordered to get partially undressed.

But, as you can see,

ours are quite frilly,

and on **YOU**, Major Trump,
they'd look RATHER silly!"

"Gorillas!" called Noah.

"You strut your stuff!"

"With pleasure – we like them with feathers and fluff.

And these, our favourites, have sequined bits,

for that extra spark of glamour and glitz!"

"Sadly, no, for we wear
super-strength drawers,
So they don't get caught on our
super-sharp
claws."

"Silly me," said Noah, "that's right, of course . . .
Well, perhaps YOU can help, Mr and Mrs Horse?"

"Good gracious, no, for you see, we're afraid
Ours are **organic, recycled . . .**
handmade."

On through the day went
the underpants parade,
Till every animal
on board had displayed.

Spotty and stripy and sporty
and suede,
Itchy and scratchy
and fussy
and frayed.

"Alas! It's no good!" Major Trump wailed.
"We've searched high and low,
admit it, we've failed!"

"That seems to be true,"
Noah agreed in despair.
"I'm really not sure
WHAT you can wear!"

"I'll be the only creature
without underpants,
From the buffaloes and bears
to the beetles and ants!

What will become of me?" Trump sobbed with a sneeze.

"Hear that? I'm ALREADY starting to
FREEZE!"

"Now, now," soothed Mrs Trump,

"Let's retrace our tracks,

And be sure to consider all of the facts."

"Well, last night my pants
went in the washing machine,
So they'd come out this morning
all fresh and clean ...

... But when I got up and checked, they were gone,
I never even put the clean ones on.

It appears there is an underpants snatcher,
But I want to be the underpants CATCHER!"

Just then there was heard a "tum-te-te-tum"
A "twiddle-de-dee" and a
"rum-pum-pum-pum".

"Mrs Noah?" cried Noah.

"Why, where have you been?"

"Oh, down below deck, having a good clean ...

… and just look at this most excellent duster,
The floors and the windows are gleaming with lustre.
It's a **godsend** indeed, though I have no idea,
How in **heaven** or **earth** it came to be here!"

The Trumps were the first
to burst into laughter,
But Noah and the animals
soon followed after.
They whooped
and they **wailed**
and caused such a
commotion,

The ark **wibbled** and **wobbled** along on the ocean.

Mrs Noah soon made Major Trump a new pair,

And then several more to put by as spare.

For as Major Trump said,

"You all **MUST** be aware . . .

...an elephant NEVER forgets...

...his own
underwear!"